Manasa Krishnakumar

To order additional copies of this book, contact:
Xlibris
1-888-795-4274
www.Xlibris.com
Orders@Xlibris.com

ISBN: Softcover   978-1-9845-7723-8
        EBook   978-1-9845-7722-1

Print information available on the last page

Rev. date: 05/01/2020

Our hero, Super Cat, has just returned to Catville, after defeating Frankenmouse and has stopped him from destroying cat kind!

Just when he arrives, his neighbor Mrs.Fuzzypaws flies through the front door screaming! Placing his cup of tea on the table, he jumps up and exclaims, "Mrs. Fuzzypaws, what happened?!"

"Oh Leonard", she said, calling him by his real name, as usual, "My precious pearl necklace is missing! Please help me!"

"This is quite serious indeed! I will come over right away to see what happened."

Super Cat followed her into her house. There were paintings and books knocked down everywhere.

Mrs.Fuzzypaws began to cry. "They've ruined everything," she wailed.

"Don't worry Mrs.Fuzzypaws, I will find your necklace," Super Cat replied.

Super Cat used his magical eyes to see what nobody else could. He scanned the scene. After a while, he found something on a bookshelf. It was a pawprint of a mouse!

"Ah, ha! This must be Melvin the mouse!" Super Cat exclaimed. "That evil mouse must have stolen your necklace! I will prepare to go to his hideout in New Moon City."

Super Cat had dealt with Melvin before and knew that it was not going to be an easy task. Melvin was always prepared for anything. Super Cat started to fly to New Moon City. He dove through busy streets and duck through alleys until he made it.

There was a small wooden box in an alley. Super cat pushed it and behold! There was a tunnel! Super cat slipped through the tunnel with difficulty, because it was for tiny mice and entered the hidden cave.

He snooped around and saw a mirror on a large wooden crate. It was Melvin's magic mirror. Super Cat quickly grabbed it. The alarms went off, and before he could escape, he was caught! Melvin's spies had caught him. He was dragged towards Melvin.

"Ha, Ha, Ha!" Melvin cackled. "Well, Well, Well, what do we have here?"

"Melvin, where is the pearl necklace?" Super Cat asked.

"I will tell you, if you give me my magic mirror," Melvin replied.

"How can I be sure you will tell me?" Super cat asked suspiciously.

"I will, on my honor as a mouse," Melvin replied impatiently.

"Fine, here you go," Super cat said, handing the mirror to Melvin.

"Ha, Ha, Ha, how could you be so foolish, Super Cat! I will never tell you where it is. Boys, take him away," Melvin demanded.

Boom! Super Cat broke out of the mice's grip. He flew towards the ceiling and lunged towards Melvin. Before Melvin could react, Super Cat sent him flying across the floor with a whack, grabbed the mirror, and flew downstairs.

While trying to find his way out, Super Cat was creating havoc. Finally, he made it outside. And with a flick of his paw slammed the entrance, locking it from the outside. He took Melvin's magic mirror and held it in the air.

"Success! Now I must investigate," He rubbed the mirror and set it down.

"Oh, Super Cat, what you want is under you," The mirror said. His claws zooming, Super Cat began digging. There it was, the shiny pearl necklace. He snatched it and flew into the air before the alarms went off again. When they did, Melvin ran out with his gang. He glared at Super cat.

"This isn't over, Super Cat!" He shouted.

Super Cat flew back home to Catville. He ran into Mrs. Fuzzypaws's house and gave her the necklace.

"Thank you so much Leonard," She said. She was so glad to have her necklace back at last!

"You are very welcome," Super Cat said. "Now it's time for tea!"

Printed in the United States
By Bookmasters